This Joey Is No Kangaroo.

He's a Bossy Aussie From Down Under.

# CONTENTS

# Real Heroes Read!

realheroesread.com

#10: Joey Down Under

David Anthony
and
Charles David Clasman

Illustrations
Lys Blakeslee

# Traverse City, MI

# Home of the Heroes

abigail

andrew

zoë

# CHAPTER 1:
# MEET THE HEROES

Welcome to Traverse City, Michigan, population 18,000. The city has everything you might expect: malls, movie theaters, schools, and playgrounds. Kids swim here in the summer and build snowmen during the winter. Sometimes they pretend that they live in an ordinary place.

But Traverse City is far from ordinary. It is set on one of the Great Lakes and attracts tourists in every season. Thousands of people visit every year.

Still, few of them know the city's real secret. Even fewer talk about it. You see, Traverse City is home to three juvenile superheroes. This story is about them.

Meet Abigail, the oldest of our heroes by a whole eight minutes. When it comes to sports, she can't be beat—not at judo, not at the javelin toss, and certainly not at jet skiing. That's right, she's the champ on land and sea. Don't even think about challenging her to a yacht race around Mackinac Island.

Andrew comes next. He's Abigail's twin brother, younger by a measly eight minutes. If it has wheels, Andrew can ride it. From jeeps to jumbo jets, he can jam, jump, and jive on one wheel or one hundred. Not even horse-drawn wagons are safe from his skating skill.

Last but definitely not least is Baby Zoë. She's proof that big things can come in small packages. She still wears a diaper, but she knows the justice system inside and out. Villains, beware! Zoë puts the *judge* in *judgment*.

Together these three heroes keep the streets and neighborhoods of Traverse City, Michigan, and America safe. Together they are …

# CHAPTER 2:
# BABY ON BOARD

"Jealous," Zoë said, crossing her arms and making a sour face.

Being a superhero, you see, didn't stop her from behaving like a toddler. Or *mis*behaving like one. She could pout as good as anyone.

As good, that is, only a whole lot louder.

Today, however, Zoë thought she had reason to pout. She and her family were on a ferry crossing Lake Huron. The crossing took about 15 minutes and would take them to Mackinac Island.

What a fun place! Zoë could hardly wait to get there. Eighty percent of the island was a historic national park. Tourists could explore its limestone caves, visit a real frontier fort, and peer through legendary Arch Rock.

In fact, Zoë had already done that. As an infant, she had flown up to Arch Rock and given the other tourists quite a scare.

So why was Zoë pouting? Because her brother got to drive the boat across Lake Huron. He always got to drive. If it had wheels, he could ride it. That went for driving boats, too.

Andrew gripped the steering wheel like the captain of a Caribbean pirate ship. Look out, Captain Jack. Here comes Admiral Andrew.

Normally the heroes and their parents didn't give in to pouting. That was a family rule. But they were on vacation and today was special. They could overlook bad behavior this once.

Mom and Dad nodded. "Keep both hands on the wheel," they told Zoë. "And don't go too fast."

Zoë clapped her hands and squealed. "Joy!" Finally a chance to drive! She shoved Andrew out of the way and grasped the wheel.

Would she drive too fast? Not for her. Zoë could fly to the North Pole and back in minutes. No speed was too fast for her.

The other passengers, however, didn't quite agree.

"I'm feeling seasick," someone in the back complained.

"Joker," Zoë replied. Think about it. They were on a lake, not the sea. How could a passenger be *sea*sick? Water-weary, maybe. But seasick? Impossible.

Next someone who lived in an apartment building would complain of having cabin fever. Funny, funny.

"Land ahoy," Dad mumbled, a hand covering his mouth. His cheeks looked a little green. Maybe he had a case of boating bloating. Zoë couldn't figure it out.

Fortunately, he and the other passengers quickly recovered. Thanks to Zoë, they had reached Mackinac Island in record time. A day of shopping, sightseeing, and sun awaited them. Who wouldn't feel better knowing that?

What they didn't know was that a surprise also awaited them. Australian Days had come to the island, and they didn't plan on leaving.

# CHAPTER 3:
# PARADE DOWN UNDER

Mackinac Island! They were finally there. As soon as the heroes and their parents disembarked, the kids started talking excitedly.

"Let's rent bicycles," Andrew suggested.

"No, let's jog around the whole island," Abigail countered.

Mom smiled and shook her head. "We'll do it all," she said. "But first, look down the street. Is that a parade coming our way?"

A parade! The heroes immediately forgot about everything else.

"Jamboree!" they exclaimed together.

The parade plodded slowly down Market Street. Floats frolicked, musicians marched, dancers dazzled, and balloons bounced.

Sounds like the average parade, right? Like the kind seen on the Fourth of July. Wrong. This parade was different. Its participants weren't people. They were animals from Australia.

Crocodiles pulled the floats while cuddly koala bears cast candy treats into the crowd.

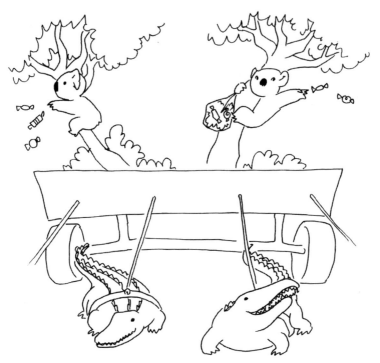

Duck-billed platypuses performed the Sydney Shuffle.

Tasmanian "dare" devils wowed the crowd by doing wheelies on their bikes.

A mob of kangaroos made much to-do by shadowboxing and socking the air.

"How cute," Abigail said. "Even the baby kangaroo is boxing."

Zoë shot her older sister a surprised look. "Joey," she corrected. A baby kangaroo was called a joey.

Abigail shrugged but didn't have time to speak. A new voice interrupted.

"Joey! That's me," the voice cried happily. "I'm Joey Down Under. How nice to meet you!"

The heroes blinked at the speaker. He was the only person in the parade. He was also Zoë's age and riding in the pouch of a mommy kangaroo.

Could this parade get any more unusual?

# CHAPTER 4:
# FORT MACKINAC MYSTERY

For a moment, everyone on Market Street went silent. They couldn't believe their eyes. Were they really seeing a parade of Australian animals? Was the leader riding in a kangaroo's pouch? Was his name Joey?

"Smile, everyone, smile," Joey said. "Welcome to Mackinac Island. G'day!"

The answers were yes, yes, and yes. Joey and his parade were real.

"Follow us," he beckoned, waving a boomerang like a music conductor waving a baton. "We're going to Fort Mackinac. There is a surprise waiting for you there."

Fort Mackinac was built in the 1700s during the American Revolutionary War. It was a British outpost until 1796, 15 years after the war. Today the fort is a museum and an official National Historic Landmark. 14 of the original buildings still stand, along with a functional 1841 canon that is fired several times a day!

Standing in front of Fort Mackinac made the heroes feel like time travelers. History had come to life before their eyes.

Even so, they couldn't forget Joey's promise. A surprise awaited them inside the fort. Each of them had a different idea of what it might be.

Abigail was sure it would be her favorite movie star, Hugh Jackman. He was from Australia just like Joey. They could be friends! More important, Mr. Jackman played Wolverine, her favorite comic book superhero.

Just imagine having claws like his.

Naturally, Andrew thought the surprise would be round. He always had wheels on his mind. He did, however, put an Australian spin on the thought. Hedgehogs, lots of them, all spinning like buzz saws. He had seen that in one of his favorite video games and wanted to join in on the fun.

"Jester," Zoë said, naming her idea.

Maybe it didn't sound very Australian. But give a wallaby a fake red nose, a silly hat, and some juggling balls. Walla! There *be* a wallaby to entertain everyone on the island like a medieval jester.

Not to mention that its feet were already the size of clown shoes.

"Stand back, mates!" Joey shouted. "Let my friends open the door."

Two burly crocodiles slithered forward, hissing at the crowd. They snatched the fort's door handles in their jaws and pulled.

"Behold!" Joey cheered as the doors opened. "I present Bang-a-roo, the boxing champion of the world."

The crowd gasped. Inside the fort was a boxing ring. In the ring stood the toughest-looking kangaroo any of them had ever seen. It had muscles on its muscles, a handlebar mustache, and boxing gloves.

The sight of it caused even athletic Abigail to step back. What exactly did Joey have planned?

# CHAPTER 5:
# DAD VS. BANG-A-ROO

Ding, ding. Dingo! Joey's plan was exactly what it seemed to be. He wanted someone from the crowd to box with Bang-a-roo the kangaroo.

Crazy! A boxing kangaroo! Who did it practice against—the Kung Fu Kitties?*

"Step right up," Joey said. "Whoever beats Bang-a-roo will win a free trip to the Australian Outback."

*See Heroes A2Z #11: Kung Fu Kitties

The first person to volunteer shocked the heroes. Dad stepped forward and thrust his fists into the air.

"I know all about boxing," he said. "I studied it when I was a teenager."

He sounded serious, but he didn't say exactly *where* he had studied boxing. It hadn't been at school or the local gym. He had studied it at a movie theater, watching all-night triple features.

Amazed as they were, the heroes tried to be supportive. They huddled around Dad in his corner of the ring and offered advice.

"Keep your wheels turning," Andrew said. "Make it hard for that kangaroo to hit you."

Abigail agreed. "Bob and weave. Duck and dodge. Don't stay in one place long."

Zoë listened carefully and wanted to help. The problem was, she didn't know much about boxing.

"Jab," she said, reminding Dad to punch. It was all she could think of to say.

Suddenly Dad sprang to his feet. "I'm ready," he said. "Let's do this." He raised his gloves like a real boxer and started stalking across the ring.

In the opposite corner, Bang-a-roo also raised its gloves. Then it raised its tail, on which it wore a third glove.

"No fair!" Abigail cried. "That's three gloves against two."

She didn't need to be Abigail Algebra to add up those odds. Dad was on the wrong side of the equation. He was outnumbered!

Dad winked over his shoulder at her.

"Don't worry," he said. "I'll swing twice as fast. My gloves will fight like four."

Abigail nodded and forced a smile. "Less math," she wanted to say. "More boxing." But the fight began with a bang.

*Bang!* That sounded more like a thump. *Thump!*

Dad and Bang-a-roo met in the center of the ring. The kangaroo's tail swatted Dad on the head and held him in place. It was like big brother versus little. Dad couldn't connect, and Bang-a-roo wouldn't let go.

True to his word, Dad swung fast. He spun his arms like windmills. Had Bang-a-roo not been holding him down, he might have floated into the clouds.

Up. Goes. Daddy.

Yet when Bang-a-roo finally let go, there was only one cloud. A cloud of dust. Fists and feet occasionally popped out, but the actual boxing match could not be seen.

When the dust had settled, the matched ended the way it started—with another thump. Dad connected on the final hit. *Thump!* His backside hit the ground.

"One!" Joey shouted with glee, playing the part of the referee. "Two!" He grabbed one of Bang-a-roo's gloves. "Three!" He raised his arm victoriously. The kangaroo's came up with his.

"I declare Bang-a-roo the winner," he cheered. "Are there any other challengers?"

Abigail nodded again, but this time she didn't smile.

"Me," she said. "I challenge. "No one beats up my Dad."

Next up: the title bout. Abigail the Athlete versus Bang-a-roo the Kangaroo. You won't want to miss this!

# CHAPTER 6:
# THE BOOT

Abigail strapped on her boxing gloves. For her, this was as natural as pulling on a pair of mittens in the wintertime. She was Triple-A, the All-American Athlete. Sports were her thing, and she was king in and out of the boxing ring.

Joey knew this, and he was prepared.

"Let's make this fair," he said. "Abigail is a sports superstar. Bang-a-roo doesn't stand a chance." He paused and raised his boomerang. "Without this," he added. "Watch!"

He hurled his boomerang at Bang-a-roo. *Bonk!* And connected with a direct hit to the kangaroo's head.

"Jerk!" Zoë gasped. How mean! How could Joey be so cruel?

The whole crowd gasped in agreement with Zoë. Boomerangs didn't belong in boxing. In fact, the only one who wasn't upset was Bang-a-roo.

The kangaroo stood calmly. And then it started to grow.

And grow.

And grow.

It grew into a giant kangaroo 20 feet tall with metal plates and armor like a cyborg from Down Under.

Joey caught the returning boomerang and cackled. "Mighty Mech-a-roo stands in the black and blue corner weighing 2 tons. It has a record of 1,009 wins and 0 losses. Incredibly, all of its victories have been knockouts. No one can stand against it."

He paused before turning to Abigail. Even she swallowed nervously in the silence.

"Abigail trembles in the red, white, and blue corner," Joey continued. "She weighs 60 pounds soaking wet. Once she cried while sitting on Santa's lap.* Good luck, so-called superhero!"

*See Heroes A²Z #8: Holiday Holdup

The crowd gasped again. Careful there, Joey. Mech-a-roo might be big and made mostly of metal, but Abigail remained the champ. She was boxing's best. She was the Princess of Prizefighting. The Ruler of the Ring. She was—

*Zoom!*

—not waiting for Joey to ring the bell.

As soon as he finished the introductions, Abigail charged. She led with her fists and didn't look down. Especially not when she jumped.

*Wham!*

And landed a double-fisted blow under Mech-a-roo's chin.

Mech-a-roo teetered briefly and then fell like a tree. One punch from Abigail was all it took.

The crowd went wild. They clapped and cheered. Abigail bowed to her left and right. She was still the champ. Had there really ever been any doubt?

Only Joey didn't celebrate. He had revenge on his mind. He might look like a nice boy from Australia, but there was something different about him.

"Give her the boot!" he shouted at Mech-a-roo. Then he flung his boomerang again.

*Bonk!* The shot struck the robotic kangaroo and it immediately came back to life. It drew back one huge foot and kicked Abigail in the pants.

*Punt!*

43

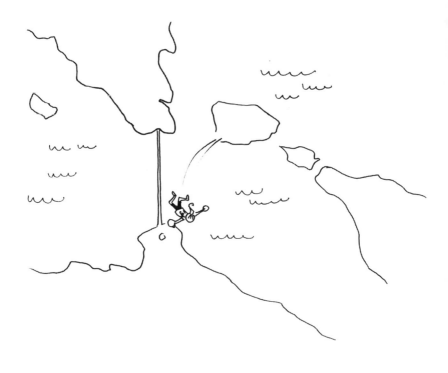

Abigail went flying. Out of the ring. Over the wall of the fort. Above the island. And across Lake Michigan.

She landed in Mackinaw City on the mainland of Michigan. The kangaroo's kick had punted her almost 3 miles! Worst of all, Andrew and Zoë were on their own. They would have to knock out Mech-a-roo without her.

# CHAPTER 7:
# THE BOOMERANG BONK

Andrew peeled out and raced into the boxing ring. Something wasn't right here. Something wasn't fair. Abigail had never lost in sports before. How could she have lost today?

"What's going on, Joey?" he demanded. "Abigail can't lose at sports. Not in a fair fight. That's her superpower."

Joey shrugged innocently, but hid the boomerang behind his back. "I guess she's not as good as you thought."

Andrew's eyes widened. "It's that boomerang! You're using it to cheat!"

"Sorry, mate," Joey said, but he didn't sound very sorry. In fact, he was grinning. "It's true, but I can't allow you to muck up my plans."

Still grinning, he threw his boomerang again. But not at Andrew or Zoë. Not at even Mech-a-roo. This time he threw it at Dad. *Bonk!* A direct hit. Then it ricocheted over to Mom and struck her, too. Double *bonk!*

Mom and Dad blinked in bewilderment. They wore dazed expressions on their faces.

"Mom? Dad?" Andrew called to them. "Are you all right?" He made a quick U-turn and started speeding toward them.

That's when Mech-a-roo struck again. It had been waiting for exactly this moment.

Out shot its foot for a second kick. *Punt!* That sent Andrew soaring after his twin sister.

Zoë watched him sail away, wondering what she should do first. Should she rescue her siblings? Save Mom and Dad? Or should she stop Joey from causing more harm?

While she wondered, Joey attacked. He was not one to waste time in thought. He threw left. *Bonk!* Then right. *Bonk!* His boomerang bopped all the bystanders goodbye.

Goodbye! Why? Because that boomerang was sly. Whatever it struck didn't break. It ducked.

For real! When the boomerang struck, the person it hit blinked the way Mom and Dad had, bewildered and confused. Then the person turned into a duck-billed platypus.

*Bonk!* Or a koala bear.

*Bonk!* Or a wallaby.

*Bonk!* Or some other animal from Australia.

49

In almost no time, Fort Mackinac looked like the Australian Outback. A Tasmanian devil dallied here, a platypus played there.

Zoë tried to keep up with the changes. Who was where and what they became. Mom and Dad were turned into koala bears. A family of four became wallabies.

Soon it overwhelmed her. The changes happened too fast. The boomerang flew even faster. She watched it whirl to and fro, but then lost sight of it in a crowd of animals. When she saw it again, it was too late.

*Bonk!*

Zoë was hit! She blinked and felt light-headed. But she didn't turn into an animal. Something different happened to her.

# CHAPTER 8:
# ZOË LOVES JOEY

Zoë loved Joey. She loved everything about him. She loved the way he talked. The way he dressed. She even loved the way he rode in a kangaroo's pouch.

Truth be told, she couldn't help herself. The decision wasn't hers. Zoë loved Joey. The boomerang made her do it.

"Joined," she cooed. In her mind, she and Joey were a couple.

Joey's boomerang, you see, was more than just a toy. It was very old and powerful. He had discovered it in the Australian Outback.

Now the toy toyed with him. How his life had changed! He wasn't a playful toddler anymore. He was a plotting tyrant looking to take over the world.

His plan: one island at a time. State by state. Country by country. The world would be his. The world would become one gigantic Australia.

That was what the boomerang wanted. So that was what Joey wanted. Like Zoë, he couldn't help himself.

His plan was in motion and already working. Conquer Mackinac Island. Check. Turn its people into animals. Check, check. Defeat the heroes and capture Baby Zoë. Check, check, and check.

But he wanted to be sure.

"Zoë, what would you like for lunch?" he asked as they walked along the beach.

"Junk food," she answered, which wasn't like her. She knew that superheroes needed to eat a healthy diet. Junk food wouldn't keep her strong.

"And for dessert?" Joey asked.

"Jellybeans," replied Zoë.

Yes! More junk food. Zoë was right where Joey wanted her. She wasn't thinking like a super-hero. She was thinking like an animal, same as everyone else on the island.

Joey smiled to himself. Zoë was thinking like a lovesick puppy. Good girl!

In fact, Joey was smiling so much that he decided to have some fun. So he and Zoë really did eat lunch. They dined at the world-famous Grand Hotel. Built in the 1800s, the hotel claims to have the longest porch in the world. Several presidents had stayed there, and the American author Mark Twain had been a frequent guest.

"What would you like to drink?" Joey asked Zoë.

"Juice," she responded.

"What flavor potato chips?"

"Jalapeño."

"And for background music?"

"Jazz."

Zoë had a quick answer for every question, but only Joey was on her mind. The Grand Hotel could sink into Lake Michigan and she wouldn't notice. She was completely under Joey's control.

Check.

# CHAPTER 9:
# CROSSING THE HURON

Back on the Michigan mainland, Abigail spun helplessly through the air.

*"Tiiimmmeee Ooouuut!"* she wailed. Colors and shapes whirled past her in a blur. Something blue, something long, something coming up fast.

*Crash-boing! Crash-boing! CRASH!*

She landed three times, bouncing in between. Metal clanged and clashed in her ears.

"Did anyone get the license plate of that kangaroo?" she mumbled. Luckily, her duffel bag had broken her fall.

Andrew was even luckier. Seconds later, he crashed where Abigail had landed. Her bag broke most of his fall. She broke the rest.

"Get off!" Abigail groaned, their noses almost touching.

"Hey, what are you doing down there?" he grinned at her.

She shoved him in the chest, and they both sat up. More metal jingled as they moved.

Metal? *Huh?* Their eyes widened in surprise. The twins were wearing silver suits of armor like old-fashioned knights.

Andrew and Abigail had crashed-landed in a shop called Medieval Knights in Mackinaw City, Michigan. Fortunately for them, the shop was one of their favorites. Everything sold there had a Middle Ages theme.

"You look ridiculous," Abigail told her brother. Both of them had been dressed accidentally in armor.

"So do you," Andrew replied. "Who ever heard of a girl knight?"

Like Zoë, Abigail needed just one word to make an excellent point. "Joan," she said, meaning Joan of Arc. She was a famous French girl who led an army to many victories in the Middle Ages.

"Whatever," Andrew replied, removing his armor. "Quit playing dress-up. This is serious. We have to get back to the island."

Abigail rolled her eyes, and then they both rolled back to the lakeshore. Crossing Lake Huron wouldn't be easy. Every boat, canoe, and raft along the shore was underwater. They had been sunk! Boomerang-shaped holes in their hulls explained how. Joey had been here earlier.

"How will we get across?" Andrew wondered. "I'm a spinner, not a swimmer."

"With this," Abigail said, reaching into her duffel bag. Almost no piece of sporting gear was too big to fit inside the bag, yet it never weighed her down. First she pulled out two rubber paddles, then an inflatable raft.

"How did you get those in there?" Andrew asked. "Playing at the beach isn't a sport."

"No, but whitewater rafting is," Abigail countered. "Now get in and paddle."

Andrew did as he was told. He got in the raft.
Simple. He started to paddle. Trouble. Andrew
knew wheels, not rafts. Whichever way he paddled,
the raft went in circles.

"We're supposed to go straight," Abigail
teased. "Mackinac Island is that way."

She raised her paddle out of the water to point,
and the most surprising thing happened. Something
leaped out of the lake and bit her paddle in half.

*Chomp!*

Then the something vanished back into the
water.

"Did you see that?" Abigail exclaimed, leaning over the edge of the raft.

Andrew grabbed her by the shoulders and yanked her safely into the raft. "Are you crazy?" he shouted. "Whatever that was will bite you next!"

Abigail gulped, and the twins peered into the lake. What they saw made them move to the middle of the raft. There wasn't just one some-thing in the water. There were a dozen somethings, maybe more. They circled the boat like hungry sharks. The heroes were surrounded!

# CHAPTER 10:
# CROCODIALS

"Crocodiles!" Andrew gasped. "Where did they come from?"

"Not crocodiles," Abigail said.

"Alligators—whatever," Andrew snapped impatiently.

Abigail shook her head. "No. Croco*dials*. Look at their backs."

He did and blinked. The crocodiles had dials! They had keys on their backs like wind-up toys. They really were croco*dials*.

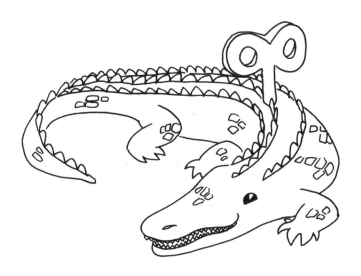

And they were hungry. The crocodials circled closer. Their metal bodies thumped and bumped against the raft. Then—*CHOMP!*—one of them spread its huge jaws and sank its teeth into the rubber. Air started leaking out of the hole immediately. The whole raft sagged.

"We have to get out of here!" Andrew cried. "What else is in your bag?"

Abigail answered by pulling out a pogo stick. "Quick! Get on my shoulders," she ordered.

As Andrew scrambled up, Abigail sprang onto the stick and bounced out of the boat. So long, leak. Hello, teeth!

*Boing!*

Abigail launched high into the air. Pogoing might not be an Olympic sport, but she rode her stick like a gold medal winner.

"Where are we going to land?" Andrew wailed. Their choices were water, raft, or crocodial.

"Keep your hands and feet inside the vehicle," Abigail said. Then the pogo stick started to drop.

*"Nooooo!"* Andrew howled even louder. A warning like Abigail's could mean only one thing at a time like this. They were going to land on a crocodial.

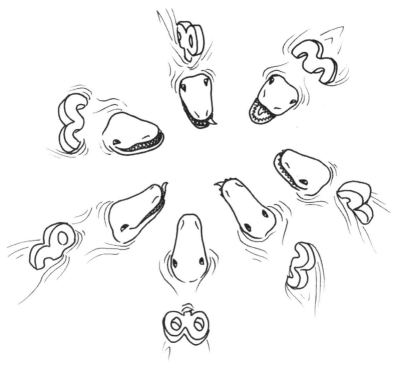

The pogo stick plummeted downward. Andrew screamed, and Abigail held her breath. She had to time their landing just right. The last thing they both saw before impact were rows of shiny teeth in an open, hungry mouth.

*Chomp!*

The mouth clamped shut and grazed Andrew's swim trunks. Any closer and he would have been feeling a breeze.

"Abigail!" he yowled, squeezing his eyes shut. That was close. Too close! Almost air-conditioned close.

Suddenly the pogo stick hit something solid. Andrew's stomach lurched into his mouth. Then he and Abigail reversed course. Up they flew instead of falling.

*Boing!*

"Whee!" Abigail cried. "This is just like Mom's favorite video game."

*Boing!* They bounced again. *Boing!* And again.

Video game? Andrew pried his eyes open and finally caught on. Abigail wasn't aiming for teeth. She was bouncing on backs, just like the little frog that hopped on crocodiles in order to cross the river.

*Boing!* After another bounce Mackinac Island come into focus. The twins were making real progress! They could almost make out the features of someone on the shore.

"Almost there," Abigail said. "Just a couple more hops."

Andrew took that as his cue. He leaped off Abigail's shoulders and onto his skateboard. He hit the nearest crocodial's back and used its tail as a ramp.

*Whoosh!*

"Showoff!" Abigail grinned, and the race was on. Sports versus wheels, sister versus brother. Who would win this summer's Crocodial Mile?

*Boing!* Abigail bounced. *Whoosh!* Andrew rolled.

Meanwhile the crocodials thrashed and gnashed their teeth. They chomped and snapped without relief. The heroes were too fast.

*Thud!* So fast that they reached the beach at exactly the same time. What a finish! They rolled onto their backs to catch their breath and gazed into the sky.

Zoë floated above them.

"Journey," she said, waving for her siblings to follow.

So the twins climbed back to their feet. They didn't know that Zoë had been struck by Joey's boomerang. They didn't know that Zoë was their enemy.

# CHAPTER 11:
# ANIMAL ARMY

"Zoë!" Andrew exclaimed. "You're okay!"

"Where's Mom and Dad?" Abigail asked. "Are they safe? Where's Joey?"

Zoë touched a finger to her lips. *Shhh.* She pointed two fingers at her eyes and then into the distance. The twins squinted. Farther inland, they spotted a group of figures marching steadily toward them. The figures were too short to be adults. They stood about as tall as kids.

"Are those koala bears?" Abigail wondered.
"Carrying spears?"

Sure enough, they were. The day couldn't
get weirder. First an all-Australian animal parade had
invaded the island. Now a marching Aussie army.

Slowly the trio of heroes crept along the
shoreline. They passed several groups of Australian animals. Some carried spears, others nets and
ropes. All of them marched toward the docks as if
preparing to leave the island.

"Wait," Andrew hissed, stopping and raising a hand. He pointed at a pair of nearby koala bears. "Is it me, or do those two look familiar?"

Abigail looked, blinked, and looked again. "Is that Mom and Dad?" she whispered in disbelief.

The koalas resembled their parents. The similarities were unmistakable. One of the bears even wore a goatee and glasses like Dad.

Zoë shrugged, pretending not to care. Only she knew the truth. The pair of koala bears were their parents, and she had to get her siblings away from them. Joey was counting on her. She couldn't let the twins find out what had been done. Not yet anyway.

Moving fast, Zoë led the twins to a cave called Devil's Kitchen. Soot blackened its interior, which is how it earned its spooky name. Many tourists stopped at the cave to take photographs. It had never been very deep. Earlier that day, however, Zoë had enlarged the cave. While Abigail and Andrew had been paddling across Lake Huron, she had been digging.

"Jailbird," she said, pointing into the now deep and dark cave. Her siblings understood. At least they thought they did.

"Joey is in there?" Andrew said.

"You captured him?" asked Abigail.

Zoë nodded—a lie. Joey wasn't in the cave. No one was … yet.

"Jaunt," she said, meaning just a little farther.

Andrew and Abigail started into the cave. No thought of danger crossed their minds. Zoë had never tricked them before. Why should they doubt her now?

"You coming?" Abigail asked, glancing over her shoulder.

No, Zoë wasn't coming. She stood outside Devil's Kitchen, hoisting a slab of limestone over her head. The slab was as long as a pick-up truck. It was just the right size.

She slammed it over the entrance to the cave, and everything went black inside. Andrew and Abigail were trapped.

# CHAPTER 12:
# THE TWIN TOSS

*Bam! Bam! Bam!*

Andrew pounded his fists against the limestone slab. He couldn't believe what had happened. Zoë had trapped him and Abigail inside a cave.

"Zoë!" he bellowed. "Let us out right now. Do you hear me?" He hoped that trying to sound like Dad would help.

It didn't.

"Quit yelling," Abigail said. "I can't think. We need to use our heads."

Andrew snapped his fingers. "That's it!" he agreed. "Use our heads. Let's start with mine."

Quickly he picked a football helmet out of Abigail's duffel. He plunked it on his head and rapped it with his knuckles.

"Knock, knock?" he grinned.

"Who's there?" Abigail asked.

"No one."

"No one who?"

"No one wants to stay in this cave," Andrew answered. "C'mon, let's get out of here."

"Sure," Abigail said. "But how?"

"You've heard of the shot put," he replied. "It's like that. But you'll be throwing me. Call it the twin toss. You can go for the gold!"

Right away, Abigail thought about arguing. The twin toss sounded dangerous. But how often did she get an opportunity like this? Only a superhero sister could throw her brother headfirst into a rock wall and not get into trouble.

"Okay, let's do it," she said. Before Andrew could change his mind, she snatched him by a belt loop and hoisted him onto her shoulder.

"One," Abigail started counting, and Andrew
swallowed.

"Two," she continued.

"Wait—!" Andrew wailed, too late.

*"Three!"*

Abigail threw and Andrew flew—headfirst into
the limestone slab.

*SMASH!* Rock, dirt, and Andrew exploded
out of the cave.

The twins were free, but not out of danger. Before the dust settled, Zoë attacked.

"Jailbreak!" she exclaimed, shocked to see that her siblings had escaped so easily.

It was time to forget the tricks and traps. She would deal with her siblings more seriously. Without a word, she squinted and started firing. Lasers sprang from her eyes.

*Pew! Pew! Pew!*

Andrew wheeled west.  Abigail edged east.
Zoë's lasers scorched the ground in between, barely
missing them both.

"Jackrabbits!" she snarled.  Her siblings were
on the run.

*Pew! Pew! Pew!*

She kept firing, and the twins kept dodging.
Behind a rock, behind a tree.  They popped out for
only a second before Zoë fired again.  It was like a
dangerous game of whack-a-mole, and Zoë was
swinging the mallet.  How long before she clob-
bered them?

# CHAPTER 13:
# HERO VS. HERO

"Look out!" Andrew yelled, but Abigail was already moving. She hurdled a pile of driftwood and dropped flat onto her stomach.

*Pew! Pew!* Zoë's lasers blazed inches away from the tip of Abigail's ponytail. Shave and a haircut—two zaps!

"What's wrong with Zoë?" Abigail gasped.

Trapping her and Andrew in a cave had been bad. But shooting lasers at them? Unthinkable! Zoë had never used her powers to try to hurt her siblings before.

"Maybe she's sick," Andrew said. "Or being controlled. Maybe she's hypnotized."

Those answers worked for Abigail. Zoë wasn't herself. Abigail didn't need more proof.

Out of her duffel bag came two water bottles, the kind athletes use to squirt drinks into their masks or helmets. She raised them like pistols and took aim at her sister.

"Take that!" she shouted, squeezing hard. Water burst from her bottles in a gurgling rush.

Zoë frowned but didn't flinch. Water bottles! That was the best Abigail could do? Epic fail! She gulped a breath and then exhaled, blowing wintry wind into Abigail's attack. In an icy instant, the watery weapons froze and fell short. Abigail should have known that would happen.

Then again, maybe she did know.  Maybe that was her plan all along.  Keep Zoë busy so she wouldn't see what happens next.  The water bottles weren't important.  They weren't the real weapons.

Andrew was.

While Zoë was distracted, he splashed into Lake Michigan.  Quickly he changed into his super-hero identity—Kid Roll.  Then he spun out and did his best impression of a human water wheel.

*Sploo-ooosh!*

Gallons of water splashed Zoë, soaking her from nose to toes. The force of the blast slammed her onto the sand. She sat there sputtering and coughing.

Abigail ran to her side. "Are you okay? Zoë, say something!"

"Did Joey hypnotize you?" Andrew asked a moment later.

At the mention of Joey's name, Zoë raised her head. She stared in the direction of the Grand Hotel and cracked her knuckles.

"Justice," she said, and her siblings knew that the water had worked. Zoë was herself again, and Joey had better beware.

# CHAPTER 14:
# GRAND ENTRANCE AND EXIT

Zoë sniffed and hung her head. She had behaved badly, like a villain. She should be scolded and sent to bed without dessert. Bad baby!

Abigail patted her sister's wet head. "Don't feel bad, Zoë. It's not your fault. Joey made you do it."

"Yeah," Andrew said. "Like when Mom and Dad tried to make us eat Sure-Burt's ice cream.* They didn't know what they were doing."

Finally Zoë nodded. "Justification," she agreed. It hadn't been her fault. Joey had hypnotized her with his boomerang.

She hugged her siblings in gratitude.

*See Heroes A²Z #1: Alien Ice Cream

When Zoë let go of her siblings, she really let loose. Abigail and Andrew could barely keep up with her. Abigail sprinted, Andrew spun, and Zoë spread her arms and sped into the lead.

"We've got wheels!" Andrew shouted.

"We've got will!" his twin continued.

"We've got Baby Zoë's skill!" they cheered together.

All three heroes laughed until the Grand Hotel came into view. Then they got quiet, serious, and ready for business.

Normally, the Grand Hotel was an inviting, friendly place. But not today, not anymore. Its appearance had changed. Boards had been nailed over its windows. Barbed wire was coiled around the railings of its world-famous porch. Piles of sandbags surrounded the hotel on all sides.

Least inviting of all, two pythons guarded the front doors. They were large, measuring almost as long as school buses. Without needing to be told, the heroes knew the snakes' names: "No" and "Trespassing." Keep out.

"Looks like we're going to have to fight our way in," Andrew commented. Abigail nodded, but Zoë disagreed.

"Jackhammer," she said, balling her hands into fists. Then she leaped into action. With her arms stretched out, she soared toward the doors.

A moment later, Abigail caught on and cried, "Strike!" A moment after that, Zoë struck.

*Crash!* She smashed fists first into the doors of the hotel.

Wood splintered, hinges snapped, and the doors to the hotel burst in. On both sides, the snakes hissed, too surprised to move. Yet when they finally did, it was too late. Zoë had already passed. Still, their mouths opened, their fangs jutted out, and they lunged forward to bite.

*Chomp! Chomp!* Direct hit! Bull's-eye one and two. Down went the snake on the left. Out cold went the snake on the right.

In their surprise, the snakes bit each other. Then they passed out from the pain. *Yeowch!*

Andrew and Abigail bounded over the snakes and followed Zoë into the hotel lobby. They didn't encounter any more guards. Instead they found Joey sitting behind the front desk.

"G'day, mates!" he called to them. He waved cheerfully, boomerang in hand. "I'm sorry, but you're too late. My animal armies have already left."

He pointed to a bank of computer screens behind him. Each one displayed a different scene of Australian animals on the march. The animals had spread out and were attacking the Michigan mainland!

Abigail was the first to react, as usual. "Put the boomerang down, Joey," she said. "It's three against one. You can't win."

Joey shrugged, still smiling and cheerful. "Wrong, wrong, wrong. I've already won. I'm just here to say goodbye." He cocked his arm, preparing to throw. "So … goodbye!"

First again, Abigail yelled, "Get down!"

The heroes hit the floor just as Joey threw. *Whoosh!* His boomerang sliced through the air inches above their heads.

"You missed!" Andrew shouted as the boomerang circled back toward Joey. But to Andrew's amazement, Joey ducked, too. He let his boomerang whirl into a door behind him.

*Crack!* White-hot energy flashed like lightning in the center of the door. When it faded, the door continued to glow and crackle with electricity.

"G'day!" Joey said again, his smile intact. He waved a final time and then jumped headfirst toward the glowing door.

*Crack!* A second burst of energy flashed when he struck. Then he was gone. Joey had escaped!

# CHAPTER 15: OUTBACK ATTACK

The heroes stared at the door where Joey had vanished. It continued to glow, but the energy was fading.

"How could he disappear like that?" Andrew wondered. "He didn't even open the door. He went *through* it."

He and his sisters stood in the lobby of the Grand Hotel. All three rubbed their eyes in disbelief. They had watched Joey vanish like a magician without a trace. But how had he done it?

"Juju," Zoë said finally, meaning that the boomerang had power the heroes didn't understand. It had hypnotized her and turned people into animals. Now it had helped Joey escape. That was some kind of supervillain triple play. Boomerang one, two, three. He's outta there!

Suddenly Abigail gasped. "We've got more than Joey to worry about," she said. "Look!"

She pointed at the row of computer monitors on the front desk. Each screen displayed Australian animals attacking Michigan. There were three armies advancing on three different cities.

A crowd of kangaroos cornered and kicked the kids in Kalamazoo.

A troop of Tasmanian devils were totally destroying Dearborn.

And a platoon of platypuses pulverized the apartments in Port Huron.

Somebody, help!

Back in the Grand Hotel, Andrew nodded to his twin. "You're right," he said. "Joey must wait. We'll have to find him later."

The heroes didn't want to leave a villain on the loose, but they had bigger trouble. All of Michigan needed them, not just Mackinac Island. And who could tell? Maybe the armies would spread out. Maybe they would march into Ohio and Indiana. Maybe all of America was in danger.

"For Michigan!" Abigail cried.

"For the USA!" Andrew cheered.

"Jupiter!" Zoë shouted. Her siblings were thinking too small. The battle against Joey was about to become a war.

# CHAPTER 16:
# MICHIGAN JUSTICE

"Come back here as soon as you can," Abigail said, making a plan. "This is Joey's headquarters. He'll be back eventually, and so will we."

Then she was off, running like only she could. In fact, she ran harder and faster than she ever had before. She was running like a new and improved version, Abigail 2.0.

Not even Lake Michigan slowed her down. The danger was that serious. She might never be able to run so fast again.

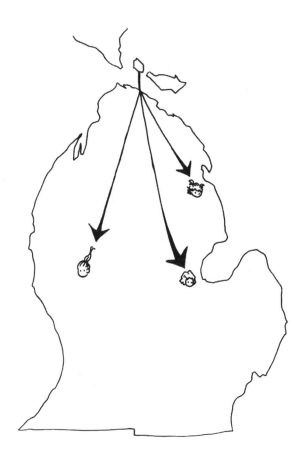

Andrew sped as close behind her as possible, racing in his Kid Roll identity. When he hit the mainland, he veered left and Abigail right. Flying overhead, Zoë banked even more sharply left.

They were three heroes splitting in three directions to battle three enemies. Doing so had worked for them before.* Let's hope it does again.

*See Heroes A²Z #9: Ivy League All-Stars

Not surprisingly, Abigail arrived at her destination first. She ran 'round Rosebush, sprinted through Stanton, and then kicked it into high gear when Kalamazoo came into view.

The kangaroo criminals weren't difficult to catch. She found them at Sutherland Park picking and kicking on kids. She skidded to a stop between the two groups and pulled a kickball from her duffel bag.

"Think you can kick?" she challenged the kangaroos. "Then play me. But be warned. I kick back."

She proved it, too, by kicking kangaroo butt. At the plate, she walloped every pitch. The kangaroos in the outfield couldn't keep up.

And on defense in the field, she was even more unstoppable. She bowled over batters and bounced out the base runners. Not one kangaroo made it home safe. The only thing that was safe was Kalamazoo.

About 130 miles east of his twin sister, Andrew rolled into Henry Ford Museum in Dearborn, Michigan. The museum celebrated cars and other vehicles of all kinds and times. It showcased presidential limousines, airplanes, antique cars, and nearly everything else with wheels. The museum was one of Andrew's favorite places to visit.

Today he was interested in the bus in which Rosa Parks had refused to give up her seat. No fair, she said. Everyone should be allowed to sit, no matter what they look like. She had used the bus to fight for equality. Now Andrew would use it to fight for justice.

Behind the wheel of brave Mrs. Parks' bus, Andrew patrolled the streets of Dearborn. He tracked Tasmanian devils down Telegraph Road and followed them up Ford Freeway. The animals tried to flee when he approached, but he lassoed every last one. Soon the bus was packed with perpetrators and parked in front of a police station.

Like Kalamazoo, Dearborn was safe again. Thank you, Andrew—and especially Rosa Parks.

Moments later, Zoë splashed down in Port Huron. The city was situated along the St. Clair River and Lake Huron. Boats and ships of all kinds filled the water, from single-person crafts to mighty freighters. Port Huron was the maritime capital of the Great Lakes.

With that in mind, Zoë went to work. She landed behind the platypus patrol and raised her voice.

"Juniors," she said, hoping to annoy the platypuses.

It worked! The platypuses heard her, snarled, and charged. Tiny animals, it seemed, didn't appreciate being called pipsqueaks.

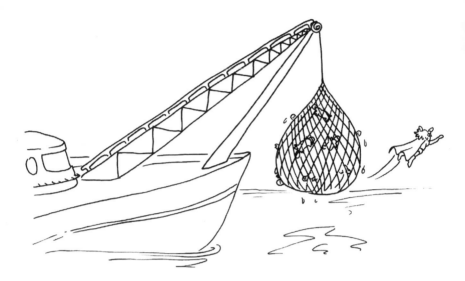

Zoë and the platypuses waded into Lake Huron. Zoë didn't use her power of flight to escape. She wanted the plats to think they could catch her. But instead, she did the catching.

*Scoop!*

A fishing net rose up out of the water. It closed over Zoë and the platypuses. At the last moment, Zoë leaped into the air and escaped.

The platypuses weren't so lucky. A crane hoisted them and the net high into the air. Trapped! The plats weren't going anywhere, and the people of Port Huron were safe.

Now the heroes could turn their attention back to Joey.

# CHAPTER 17:
# MOVING MACKINAC

Joey raised a pair of binoculars to his eyes, and the heroes came into view. They were returning to Mackinac Island, just as he knew they would. They were also heading for a big surprise. Huge, actually. Enormous.

He met them on the roof of the Grand Hotel. The higher the meeting point, the better. Abigail arrived first with her siblings close behind.

"G'day again, mates," he said, calm and unafraid. "I suppose you're here to arrest me. You'd better get on with it."

He smiled as she spoke, and even offered up his hands for cuffs. In them, he clutched his baleful boomerang.

Abigail spread her arms to keep her siblings from rushing forward. Capturing a villain was never easy. Joey was up to something.

"Drop the boomerang," she demanded.

Joey shrugged, turning the boomerang in his hands. "This old thing? I found it in the mud. Would you like me to put it back?" He raised an arm to throw.

"Don't!" Andrew shouted, realizing the danger.

"Stop!" cried Abigail.

No matter. Joey's arm came down, and the boomerang whizzed toward the ground.

The heroes were on Joey in an instant. Grab!
Clutch! Snag! They hog-tied, pinned down, and
wrapped up Joey all at the same time.

But again, no matter. Because the boomerang
struck the ground.

*KAH-BOOOOOM!*

A powerful earthquake rumbled across
Mackinac. The whole island seemed to lose its
balance and wobble from side to side. Not even
the heroes could hang on. First they lost their grips
on Joey. Then the quake tossed them aside like
fleas off a dog's back.

*Splish! Splash! Splosh!*

The heroes splashed into the waters beneath Mackinac Bridge. The 5-mile long bridge connects Michigan's Upper and Lower peninsulas. Zoë had actually borrowed a section of the bridge once before.*

Today, however, she picked up her brother and sister and set them on the bridge. Then she pointed into the distance.

"Jumbo!" she said in alarm.

Mackinac Island was moving. The earthquake hadn't been a regular earthquake. The whole island had come to life!

Mackinac was actually a gigantic sea turtle. And it was swimming right toward the heroes!

*See Heroes A²Z #2: Bowling Over Halloween

# CHAPTER 18:
# BIG TURTLE

Native Americans first discovered Mackinac Island. They named it *Mishi-mikinaak*, which meant "big turtle" in their language. To them, the island looked very much like a big turtle in the water.

Today, Joey used his boomerang to make that name more meaningful than ever. Mackinac Island really was a big turtle now.

"Have you ever seen a monster that big before?" Andrew asked in awe.

The heroes had battled a giant fudge blob, dinosaurs, and a three-headed hydra—all of them giants. But none of them had been half the size of the Mackinac Island turtle.

"Juggernaut," Zoë whispered, fearing the turtle was too big to be stopped.

Abigail shook her head, refusing to give up. "What's that in the water next to the turtle?"

Her siblings squinted. "Someone on a jet ski?" Andrew guessed.

"Juvenile?" added Zoë.

Exactly. A young person, namely Joey. He was cruising over the waves next to the turtle. He clutched the boomerang between his teeth.

"It's Joey!" Abigail cried. Then she dove off the bridge, hit the water, and started swimming like a gold medalist.

"Big mistake!" Joey snarled over the hum of the jet ski's engine. He sliced his boomerang through the air like a sword, and the turtle raised one massive flipper.

Abigail sputtered in the water. Was Joey controlling the turtle with his boomerang like a remote control? He swung his arm and the turtle copied him.

"Get the boomerang!" she yelled to her siblings. "Destroy it!"

Then the turtle's flipper raced downward and slapped her out of the water. She flew back to the bridge, crashed into its cables, and became wrapped up like a bug in a spiderweb.

Andrew rolled into action next. Among the cars and trucks parked on the bridge, he spotted an ice cream truck. Perfect! He would put Joey on ice.

"I need your truck," he told the driver.

The ice cream man took one look at Andrew and his jaw dropped. "You're Kid Roll!" he gasped. "Here, take the keys. You're my hero!"

Seconds later, Andrew copied his sister by driving off the bridge. The difference? Andrew was behind the wheel of an ice cream truck.

"Turtle tracks!" he howled, naming his favorite ice cream flavor.

Not only did he copy his twin sister's dive. He copied her result. Disaster! Andrew dove into the air, the turtle's tail hit him, and then he and the truck hit the water.

One, two, three—*splash!*

Talk about going down with the ship. Andrew was going down with the *chip.* Chocolate chip, that is, along with the vanilla and strawberry, too. What a delicious way to go!

Last but not yet a feast, Zoë zoomed after Joey. The turtle was distracted. The time to strike was now. The time to eat was soon.

She flew faster than she ever had before. Tears streamed from her eyes and froze on her cheeks in the wind. Her arms stretched. Her hands reached. Almost there. Just another inch …

Got it! Her fingertips brushed the boomerang in Joey's grasp.

"Never!" he snarled, twisting away.

Then—*CHOMP!*—the turtle recovered. It opened its mouth, caught Zoë, and swallowed. Down, down, down she tumbled into darkness.

# CHAPTER 19:
# A SNEEZY SOLUTION

"Victory!" Joey cheered, raising his boomerang in triumph. "I win!"

Across the water and sinking, Andrew scowled. "No, the boomerang won. You'd be just another baby without it."

"Like Zoë?" Joey shot back.

Andrew's scowl deepened. "Zoë is a hero because of *who* she is, not what. You could learn from her."

"But I did!" Joey laughed. "I learned that my boomerang works on you heroes. Watch!"

Still laughing, he flung the boomerang at Andrew. *Bonk!* One second Andrew was Andrew. The next he was a crocodial.

The same went for Abigail. Tangled in the cables of the Mackinac Bridge, she was helpless. All she could do was watch and scream.

"Leave my brother alone!" she wailed.

Joey laughed harder and threw his boomerang again. *Bonk!* Abigail became a crocodial, too.

"Now don't go crying crocodial tears," Joey teased.

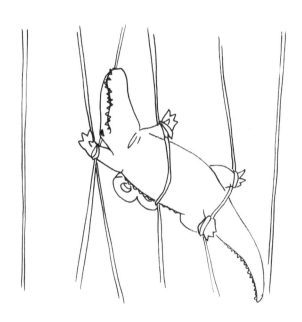

Meanwhile, Zoë found herself in the belly of the turtle. She had heard stories about people being swallowed by whales before, but never turtles. Who knew what she would discover in there?

"Jiminy" she whispered, thinking of Pinocchio and Jiminy Cricket.

After a quick search, she found nothing that could help her escape. That left her with only one option. She had to leave the way she came in. So Zoë took a deep breath and then started flying up. The light brightened as she neared the turtle's mouth, but a dark blob blocked the way out.

The uvula! That's the crazy flap of tissue that hangs from the back of your mouth. Seeing the turtle's uvula gave Zoë an idea.

A gross idea.

She darted up to the uvula and tickled it. Goochee-goochee-goo! Heavy on the goo.

What happened next was wild, wet, and windy. The turtle sneezed like a hurricane.

*Aaaah-CHOOOOO!*

Zoë and the slime in the turtle's nose and throat hurtled into the air. But Zoë didn't slow or try to fight it. She was moving faster than she could fly.

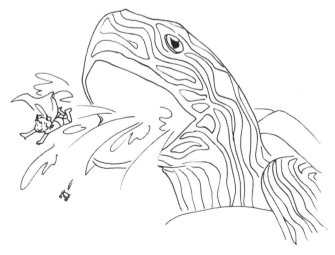

So fast, in fact, that she zipped past Joey before he realized what was happening. She even snagged the boomerang out of his hands.

"Hey!" he whined. He had lost his boomerang, and he was covered in turtle nose goo.

Zoë giggled and pointed at him. "Jellied!" she teased. Then she snapped the boomerang over her knee.

*BOO-OOM!*

Power exploded across Lake Michigan and spread rapidly away from Zoë like ripples in a pool. The power washed over Joey, the turtle, her siblings, the horizon, and beyond.

Everything it touched turned back to normal and returned to its rightful place. The giant turtle became Mackinac Island again. All of the Australian animals became people. Abigail and Andrew were themselves.

123

Even Joey's mother returned to normal. That's right, his mother! She had been the kangaroo in whose pouch he rode. It was kind of obvious now.

As for Joey, he didn't change much on the outside. He changed on the inside. He turned into an ordinary baby in a diaper, just like Andrew had said.

"Boom-boom?" he asked his mother in baby talk.

She shook her head. "I'm sorry, honey. Your boomerang is gone. But we will buy you a new toy."

The heroes decided not to press charges against Joey. The boomerang had been the real villain. So they helped repair the damage around Michigan and the island. Then they joined their parents for the rest of their well-deserved vacation.

Together they hiked, swam, shopped, and explored. But they also kept their eyes opened. A supervillain could be anyone. Even a baby in a diaper. Even furry felines in ...

Book #11:
Kung Fu Kitties

# Fighting Crime Before Bedtime

... and more!

# Connect with the Authors

Charlie:
charlie@realheroesread.com
facebook.com/charlesdavidclasman

David:
david@realheroesread.com
facebook.com/authordavidanthony

# realheroesread.com

facebook.com/realheroesread
youtube.com/realheroesread
twitter.com/realheroesread
myspace.com/realheroesread

# About the Illustrator
# Lys Blakeslee

Lys graduated from Grand Valley State University in Michigan where she earned a degree in Illustration.

She has always loved to read, and devoted much of her childhood to devouring piles of books from the library.

She lives in Wyoming, MI with her wonderful parents, two goofy cats, and one extra-loud parakeet.

# Thank you, Lys!